Fairy Cloud
Parade

FAIRY SCHOOL

Fairy Cloud Parade

by Gail Herman
illustrated by Fran Gianfriddo

A Skylark Book

New York ·Toronto·London·Sydney·Auckland

RL 2.5, 006–009

FAIRY CLOUD PARADE

A Bantam Skylark Book / June 1999

Skylark Books is a registered trademark of Bantam Books, a division of Random House, Inc. Registered in U.S. Patent and Trademark Office and elsewhere.

ISBN 0-553-48680-2

Published simultaneously in the United States and Canada

Bantam Books are published by Bantam Books, a division of Random House, Inc. Its trademark, consisting of the words "Bantam Books" and the portrayal of a rooster, is Registered in U.S. Patent and Trademark Office and in other countries. Marca Registrada. Bantam Books, 1540 Broadway, New York, New York 10036.

PRINTED IN THE UNITED STATES OF AMERICA

CWO   0 9 8 7 6 5 4 3 2 1

For Elizabeth, once again

Chapter 1

"I don't think this leaf is exactly right," said Olivia Skye, a tiny fairy three inchworms high.

"It looks perfect to me," Belinda Dentalette said.

"You're the best artist we know," added Dorrie Windmist.

"When your parents have the new fairy baby," Trina Larkspur told Olivia, "you'll be able to teach it how to paint the best sunsets and color the prettiest butterfly wings."

Olivia grinned at her three best friends. Every time she thought about her new brother or sister, she got excited. She couldn't wait to be a big fairy sister. But right now she had to be a good fairy student and get her leaf just right.

Olivia and her friends went to Fairy School, a grove of trees surrounded by a grassy meadow. They studied subjects like star polishing and rainbow sliding. Someday they would earn the glittering silver wings that grown-up fairies wore. They would slide down the Rainbow Bridge to Earth-Below to work fairy magic for the Big People there.

But that was thousands of sunsets away. Right this very minute they had leaf-making class.

Olivia walked slowly around her leaf and tucked her blond hair behind her ears. The shape was pretty, but the color seemed drab. She motioned for a nearby firefly to shed more light.

"Lime green, please," she said to a centi-

pede holding her supplies in his hundred feet. The centipede examined each paintbrush, then handed a green one to Olivia. "Thank you." Olivia carefully painted the leaf. "There!" she said, satisfied.

Belinda grinned. "That *is* nicer!"

"Maybe you can help me fix mine!" Dorrie's round face broke into a grin as she held up a lopsided leaf. "Oops!" She stumbled over the centipede and almost fell off the first-grade branch. "I'm sorry," she said to the centipede as Belinda steadied her.

"With all these little bugs helping out, it's easy to trip over someone," Olivia said gently.

Dorrie tossed her long, unruly curls and almost hit the caterpillar again. "Especially for the clumsiest fairy in school, you mean."

"You're not clumsy," Olivia said. "You're just . . . just . . ." She searched for the right words.

"Just a little awkward sometimes. Everyone

is." Trina wiped a smudge of green paint from her serious face.

Olivia smiled. Leave it to bookworm Trina to come up with the right way to say something.

"Well, I just wish my leaves wouldn't come out so lumpy," Dorrie said.

"Hmmm." A fairy named Laurel zipped over to inspect Dorrie's leaf. "It is lumpy," she agreed. "It looks like you." Then she flew away with a nasty laugh.

Dorrie's wings wilted.

"Just ignore her, Dorrie," Belinda said. "Let's talk about something else. How do you think fairy babies are born?" she asked. "I heard that each time a flower blooms, a baby fairy is waiting inside."

"I heard that storks grow fairies in eggs and deliver them to parents," Dorrie said.

"You're both right. Sort of," Trina told them. She read lots of books and knew all sorts of interesting things. "Storks grow fairy flowers in special gardens. Red flowers for boys. Yellow flowers for girls. When a fairy is ready to come out, the flower blooms and the stork delivers the baby to the waiting family. Like yours, Olivia."

Just then their teacher, Ms. Periwinkle, flew over. She hovered above Olivia's leaf. "This is wonderful work," she said. "I think we should hang it in the school meadow so everyone can see it!"

"Oh!" Olivia said softly. "Thank you!"

"And speaking of the school meadow," Ms. Periwinkle continued, "our class is supposed to go there now. Mr. Meadowleaf is about to make a special announcement."

Olivia knew Mr. Meadowleaf was the best art teacher in Fairy School. He taught only the most talented taller fairies. "Why does he want to talk to everyone?" she asked.

Ms. Periwinkle's eyes twinkled. "I can't say. But it's very exciting!"

Chapter 2

Olivia looked around the crowded meadow. "There's Mr. Meadowleaf," she told her friends.

Mr. Meadowleaf fluttered to a low-hanging branch. "Fairies!" he called. "You all know about the Fairy Cloud Parade. That's where cloud-shaping fairies pull the best clouds of the year through Fairyland. Then they take the clouds down the Rainbow Bridge and release them over Earth-Below."

"I love the Fairy Cloud Parade," Dorrie said. "The clouds are so beautiful. My family always goes to watch."

"This year is the one thousandth anniversary of the parade. And something very special has been planned. To tell you more, I have the great honor of introducing one of Fairyland's most respected cloud-shaping fairies, best known for cloud shapes like 'Bumblebees at Play' and 'Flight of the Bluebird.'"

Olivia gasped. "It's Magdalena! My very favorite artist!"

"And now," Mr. Meadowleaf continued, "I present . . . Magdalena!"

Olivia clapped frantically as Magdalena flew to the branch. "Thank you, Mr. Meadowleaf. Hello, fairies. And you too, birds and bugs." She smiled at a passing robin.

She's so nice! Olivia thought.

"This year I am the artist in charge of the Fairy Cloud Parade. And I would like to celebrate talented small fairies. So I've decided to do something we've never done before. I am happy to announce a cloud-shaping contest."

Olivia edged forward, eager to hear more.

"Contestants will shape model clouds," Magdalena explained. "And I'll choose the most original shape as the winner. Then I'll work with that fairy to sculpt the biggest cloud in Fairyland."

Olivia could barely breathe. The winner would work with Magdalena? To shape the biggest cloud? It would be Olivia's dream come true—to meet the famous artist . . . and create a beautiful cloud for everyone in Fairyland and Earth-Below to see.

Magdalena paused. "And that cloud will lead this year's Fairy Cloud Parade.

"Anyone can enter," she added before flying off the branch. "Just bring your cloud to the Fairy Hall one week from today for judging."

"Wow!" Olivia jumped with excitement.

"This is going to be so much fun." All around, fairies chattered about the contest and what their clouds would look like.

"You'd better get to work," Belinda said, nudging her. "It sounds like everyone's going to enter."

"I can't wait until you win," Dorrie said.

Olivia smiled. "I don't know if I'll win, Dorrie. There are some really talented fairies. But I can't wait to spend every minute working on my model. Imagine, Magdalena judging my cloud. It has to be perfect." As she flew back to her class branch, she started to think about what her cloud would look like.

"Attention! Attention!" A messenger fairy hovered above Ms. Periwinkle's desk. "I have a message for Olivia Skye. Your parents just got their babies. Twins!"

Chapter 3

Twins! All thoughts of the contest flew right out of Olivia's head.

"Oh my goodness!" Belinda cried, flapping in excited circles. Dorrie squealed and gave Olivia a hug.

Trina clapped her wings. "This is amazing!" she said.

"Two fairies are even better than one!" Olivia told her friends. She didn't know any fairy twins, and now she'd have a set in her very own tree-house.

Laurel faked a big yawn as she sat at her toadstool desk. "Babies are boring—and they're one big pain. They cry all night long, and those smelly leaf-diapers! I'm so glad I'm an only fairy.

"Besides," she added nastily, "if you're going to play with the babies so much, when will you have time to shape your cloud?"

"Don't you worry about Olivia," Belinda said. "She can do everything."

Olivia blushed. But really, she thought, Belinda is right about one thing. I can play with the babies *and* shape my cloud. No problem.

Ms. Periwinkle waved her wings to get the students' attention. "Congratulations on your twins, Olivia," she said as the fairies took their seats.

"Are your twins boys, girls, or one of each?" Dorrie asked.

"I have no idea!" Olivia exclaimed.

"The messenger fairy has a note from your parents saying it's okay for you to leave school early. You can go home and meet the twins right now!" Ms. Periwinkle said.

Laurel snorted. "Gee, Olivia. Tough day."

Olivia didn't pay any attention to Laurel. She was already flying away.

***

In no time at all, Olivia skidded into her treehouse.

"Hi, sweet fairy," said Mrs. Skye. She pointed to a gurgling bundle nestled in a little bed. "This is your baby sister, Natalia."

"Hi," said Olivia, suddenly feeling shy.

"And this," said Mr. Skye, flying into the room and pointing to a second bundle, "is your brother, Nicholas."

Olivia caught her breath. A girl and a boy! The twins were wrapped up tight in soft green pea pods. They wore little flower caps to keep their heads warm. Only their tiny faces peeked

out. The twins stared at Olivia with bright blue eyes.

"Oh!" she breathed. "They're just perfect." And they smelled so sweet and powdery. Olivia bent closer. She gently patted Nicholas's cheek. It felt like a puffy cloud.

"How did we get twins?" she asked.

"Well . . ." Mr. Skye settled in a moss chair, still cradling Nicholas. "Your mom and I each told a different stork we wanted a fairy."

Mrs. Skye laughed. "And neither of us knew the other had done it! So we got two. Nicholas and Natalia!"

"Twins!" Olivia sighed happily. "Can I hold one?"

"Sure," Mr. Skye said. "But first we need to put on their fairy bells."

Olivia knew that every fairy baby was given a set of fairy bells so its parents could tell where it was every single minute. Baby fairies learned to fly before they walked, and they were very fast. Without the bells, a baby fairy could fly off when its mother or father glanced away, and maybe get lost.

While Mr. Skye slipped the small silver bells over each baby's wings, he asked Olivia, "How was school today?"

"Oh!" She suddenly remembered her exciting news. "It was great. Magdalena came and announced a cloud-shaping contest for the Fairy Cloud Parade."

"Magdalena? Your favorite artist? You must be thrilled," said Mrs. Skye. "What will your cloud look like?"

"I'm not sure yet," Olivia said. "My cloud has to be special. I don't know if I'm a good enough artist to win the contest, but imagine Magdalena looking at my art! I have to find the perfect model."

Mr. and Mrs. Skye were both tree fairies who figured out how tall trees should be in forests. They used a lot of math for that. But they knew a lot about art too.

"Why don't you explore Fairyland to find something that inspires you?" Mr. Skye suggested.

"Good idea!" Olivia knew she should start her search right away. She was so particular about her art, it could take days to make her cloud just right. And she had only one week.

But still . . . Olivia bent close to Natalia and smelled her sweet breath. She hated to leave her brand-new sister and brother. I'll go in a little while, she promised herself.

Chapter 4

For the rest of the afternoon and all that evening, Olivia played with the babies. They were the cutest fairies she'd ever seen.

When she woke up the next morning, she flew into the kitchen, where Nicholas and Natalia were eating breakfast. When the babies saw Olivia, they waved their little fists and gurgled.

"Wivvy!" said Nicholas.

Olivia's eyes opened wide. "Did he just say my name?"

"Wivvy!" said Natalia.

"They both did!" Mr. Skye exclaimed. "Their first words!"

Olivia picked up both babies.

"You spent so much time with the twins yesterday, you barely ate," her mother said. "Have a glass of nectar. And Dad's going to mix up a batch of Pixie Pancakes."

"Mmm-mmm," said Olivia. "My favorite. But I'll have to eat quickly. I'm going to fly around Fairyland this morning to find a shape for my cloud."

The babies fluttered their wings, and their fairy bells pealed softly through the tree-house.

"Sounds like new babies in here," a carpenter ant said as she stepped into the house.

Mrs. Skye jumped up. "The construction crew is here!"

"What's going on?" Olivia asked as a group

of ants marched into the tree-house, carrying tiny hammers and wood-chip nails.

"They're here to build more baby furniture," Mrs. Skye explained. "We need two of everything. Two cloud-chairs for feeding, two toadstools for diaper changing . . ."

"I want to make the tree nice for the babies too," Olivia said. "I can put up magic wallpaper in their branch—the kind that shows the sun during the day and the moon at night. Then I can choose a star for a night-light. I'll have it shrunk at the Magic Minimall and hang it right above their cribs."

"What about your cloud?" asked Mrs. Skye.

"I'm not worried," Olivia said confidently. "I have plenty of time."

∗∗∗

For the rest of the weekend, Olivia puttered around the Skyes' tree, fixing up the babies' room and playing with them.

Monday morning she finally left Nicholas and Natalia to go to school.

"So are you nice to your little brother and sister?" Dorrie asked Olivia. They were in the school meadow, waiting for raindrop class to begin. Ms. Periwinkle was pulling down a few small clouds so the class could practice making showers. "My taller sister, Arianna, is too busy with her friends to pay much attention to me at all."

"The twins are too cute to ignore. And too little. But they're getting so big so fast. They're already talking. And they might fly any day now." Olivia yawned.

"No wonder you're tired, Livvy. You have so many things happening at once," Belinda said. "The babies *and* the contest."

"You must have done a lot of work over the weekend," Trina added. "What does your cloud look like?"

Olivia gulped. She hadn't had time to look

for the perfect cloud shape, let alone start her model.

Before she could explain, Ms. Periwinkle told the class to start making rain fall out of the clouds.

While the fairies practiced, Mr. Meadowleaf flew across the meadow. He spoke to Ms. Periwinkle.

"Olivia!" Ms. Periwinkle called. "Please join us for a moment."

"Uh-oh, guess who's in trouble," Laurel said with a sneer.

Olivia ignored the mean fairy. She raced to her teacher.

Mr. Meadowleaf smiled. "So this is the talented little fairy. I'm pleased to meet you, Olivia. I saw your leaf in the school meadow. Best I've seen in a long time."

"Thank you." Olivia blushed.

"You have a special talent, and I can help you improve. Would you like to join my art class?"

Olivia gulped. What an honor! She didn't know of any fairy her size who had ever been asked to join the taller fairies for art.

Mr. Meadowleaf smiled. "Are you interested?"

Olivia's eyes lit up. "Yes, yes, yes!" She could hardly believe her luck!

"Great. We'll see you in class tomorrow!"

***

Olivia didn't go to Fairyland Meadow to play with her friends after school, even though she wanted to. She had so much to do, she flew straight home. She could hear the twins shouting before she could even see her tree. For little baby fairies, she thought, they sure make a lot of noise. Mr. and Mrs. Skye were changing leaf diapers when she flew inside. The twins squirmed on the changing toadstools.

"I'm home," Olivia said. "And I've got great news!"

"You need gray shoes?" Mrs. Skye asked

23

above the racket. She turned to one wriggling baby. "Natalia, stay still for one second."

"You want to snooze?" Mr. Skye shouted. Nicholas rolled off his toadstool, and Mr. Skye scooped him up before he hit the floor.

"No, no," Olivia said loudly. She ran her fingers through Natalia's soft tufts of blond hair. Then she turned to Nicholas and kissed his bald head.

The twins immediately quieted down. "Hi, Wivvy," they both said.

Mr. and Mrs. Skye sighed, finished the diapering, and handed the babies to Olivia.

"Now we can talk," said Mrs. Skye as they all sat down. "What did you say, sweet fairy?"

Olivia bounced the twins up and down on her knees. "I said I have great news! I've been moved to a special art class."

"That's fantastic," Mr. Skye said.

"We're so proud of you," Mrs. Skye said.

"This never happened to a fairy my height. If I'm good enough to be in Mr. Meadowleaf's class, maybe Magdalena will give me some advice when she looks at my contest cloud. I just have to fly around Fairyland to find that special shape. I was thinking it could be a—"

Z-z-z-z-z. Z-z-z-z.

Olivia looked up. Had the bumblebee neighbors come to visit?

Those weren't bees. They were her parents, snoring loudly, fast asleep on the soft moss couch. They look so comfortable, Olivia thought, yawning. I could use a nap too. The twins leaned back against her. They snuggled up close, sighed, and shut their eyes.

"I can always fly around Fairyland tomorrow. . . ."

Chapter 5

The next morning, Olivia woke up early. Only four days until the contest, she thought, and still no idea for my cloud. She decided to fly slowly to school and check out all the sights.

She was about to leave the tree-house when she saw the twins eating their breakfast berries while her parents read the newspaper. She stopped to play with the babies. Just for a second, she told herself.

"Oh, look," Mrs. Skye said. "A tree lecture at the library this afternoon. How interesting."

"Too bad we can't go," Mr. Skye said. "Who would watch the twins?"

"I'll do it!" Olivia said.

"But you're such a small fairy yourself, Olivia," her mother said.

"I'm three inchworms high. That's tall enough to take care of the twins. Besides, the babies are so good when they're with me. And it's only for one afternoon."

"Well, maybe it would be all right. . . ."

"Cuckoo, cuckoo." A cuckoo-clock bird flew past their window.

"Oh, no! I'm late for school. I thought I was going to be early."

"That's how it is with babies," Mrs. Skye said, smiling. "Time flies. Have a good day, sweetie."

"Good luck in your new art class," Mr. Skye called.

Olivia rushed straight to her class branch

and got there just in time to sing the Fairy School Pledge. She sighed, upset that she hadn't had a spare second to look for a cloud idea.

Ms. Periwinkle announced, "Time for tooth fairy class! Follow me, fairies." The teacher led the class outside. She waved her wand, and the sun seemed to dim. Elsewhere in Fairyland, the sun still shone. But just above school, day was turning into night.

"Now," Ms. Periwinkle said, "I'd like you to practice flying in the dark, as real tooth fairies do."

It was black as midnight. Olivia couldn't really see the other fairies—just fuzzy outlines. But she thought the fairy right next to her was Belinda. "Belinda?" she said softly. "Can I talk to you? I'm getting worried about the cloud-shaping contest."

"Hmmm?" the fairy murmured.

"I spent all weekend playing with the twins.

I haven't started my shape yet. I don't even know what it's going to look like! But it has to be perfect for Magdalena."

"You're never going to win the contest," the other fairy whispered.

"Belinda?" Olivia was shocked. Her friend wouldn't be so mean.

"It's me—Laurel," the fairy said loudly. "And *my* cloud is going to lead the Fairy Cloud Parade."

"It is not," Olivia said angrily. "I'm going to figure out my shape this afternoon. Then I'm going to work on it every chance I get."

"That won't matter," Laurel shot back. "Aunt Magdalena is going to pick my cloud as the winner!"

Aunt Magdalena? Olivia had had no idea Laurel was related to the most famous artist in Fairyland. Maybe she would win the contest. Olivia didn't know what to say.

"Oof!" Suddenly Dorrie barreled into Laurel and sent her spinning.

"I'm sorry," Dorrie gasped. "It's hard to fly when you can't see where you're going!"

Olivia stifled a giggle. Sometimes Dorrie's mishaps turned out to be very helpful.

"Okay, class!" Ms. Periwinkle called. "I'm turning on the light."

Slowly the skies brightened. It was morning once again. Olivia could clearly see Laurel, picking herself off the ground. Laurel narrowed her eyes and sneered. "I am going to win that contest!"

"Don't worry about her," Belinda said, flying over. "She made me so crazy about being a tooth fairy, I couldn't even think straight."

"And remember, Magdalena seemed really nice," Trina put in. "She wouldn't let Laurel win the contest just because they're related."

"Do you really think so?" Olivia asked.

Her friends all nodded.

"Everything's going to be fine," Dorrie promised. "I bet you'll feel better after your special art class."

***

Olivia flew into Mr. Meadowleaf's art branch feeling a little nervous. The other fairies seemed so much taller. They were gathering supplies and setting up easels.

I hope I'm good enough to be here, she thought.

"Hello, Olivia." Mr. Meadowleaf fluttered over. "Welcome to class. Everyone is doing independent study this week. You can work on anything you want, but most fairies are working on their clouds. I imagine you're entering the contest?"

"Yes, but . . . I haven't started my shape yet."

Mr. Meadowleaf frowned. "The models are due at Fairy Hall in just a few days. We don't rush through projects at the last minute in this class."

"I know. But I can't figure out what my

cloud should look like. I want to do something really amazing to impress Magdalena. Like a castle, or a bridge, or . . ." Olivia trailed off. Mr. Meadowleaf was shaking his head.

"What's wrong?" she asked.

"The best art is about strong feelings. Maybe you should think of something more personal. Something you feel connected to."

"You mean I should think of something I love. And something that's beautiful at the same time." Olivia thought for a minute. "But what?"

"Inspiration will come to you, Olivia. That's what being an artist is all about."

"But what if it doesn't come in time?"

"Just do your best, and you'll think of something. I'm sure of it," her teacher said. "Maybe you should carry some cloud dough with you while you're thinking of ideas. Then, when something catches your eye, you can start shaping your cloud right away."

Olivia looked around the branch. All the taller fairies were hard at work. "I've got to think of something," she told herself firmly, reaching for a glob of dough. But by the end of the class, she still didn't have an idea.

Chapter 6

"We're off to the tree lecture," Mr. Skye told Olivia when she flew home, deep in thought about the contest.

"That's this afternoon?" Olivia groaned. "I forgot."

"Is it still okay, sweet fairy?" her mother asked. "We can stay home if you like."

Olivia looked at her parents, dressed up and ready to go. Then she saw Nicholas holding his arms out for her to pick him up. Natalia giggled and blew kisses.

"No, you go on," Olivia said to her parents. "And don't worry," she added. "Everything will be fine."

Mr. and Mrs. Skye kissed the twins and Olivia and flew off.

Olivia smiled at the babies. "All right, you two. You can read while I try to get inspired."

She handed the fairies a book to share. Then she took out her wad of dough.

"Wook!" Nicholas pointed to a picture of a bee, buzzing around a daisy. The babies flapped their wings, pretending to be bees. They could hover in the air for a few seconds now. Pretty soon, Olivia knew, they'd be flying all over the place.

"*Bzzzz, Bzzzzz,*" they said, excited by the game.

They kept flapping their wings and wobbling around the kitchen. Natalia brushed against a jar of nuts. *Plink, plink, plink.* Nuts clattered to the floor. Then Nicholas's wing tipped over a big bag of breakfast berries. *Plop, plop, plop.* Berries landed on top of the nuts. Olivia started to clean up, but she slipped on the nuts, slid on the berries, and fell to the floor.

"Uh-oh," said Nicholas.

The babies' wings wriggled as they tried to help Olivia. Bowls fell to the floor, and Nicholas put one on his head. Natalia reached for another. Somehow she knocked over a sack of flour. Fine white powder spilled over everything.

"Snow!" said Natalia. Excited, the babies rolled in the flour and flapped their wings as Olivia stumbled to her feet. In seconds flour coated the entire kitchen.

This calls for some fairy magic, Olivia thought. Her parents didn't like to use magic for discipline. But this was an emergency! Olivia pulled her mom's magic wand out of a drawer.

"Babies roll and babies hop, right this minute, babies stop!" Nicholas and Natalia froze where

they had been rolling on the floor. They were covered in berry juice and wore shell-bowls on their heads, but still, they looked peaceful. How long would the spell last? Olivia was just a first-grader, after all.

Nicholas blinked. Natalia stirred. They both sat up.

Quick! Olivia thought. I've got to keep them here! If they start flying again, they'll make even more of a mess.

Suddenly she spied her cloud dough. "I've got it!" She grabbed the dough and started to pinch it into shape. "Who can sit still the longest while I make a special surprise?"

"Me!"

"Me!"

Olivia's idea worked! She pinched and prodded the dough to make it look like the messy twins. Every few seconds, she stopped to show the fairies what she was doing. They sat perfectly still, watching the cloud dough take shape—the shape of two fairy babies!

"Us pwetty!" said Natalia when Olivia showed them the finished sculpture.

"Yes," Olivia agreed. "And messy too! Time to clean everything—and everybody!"

She waved for the magic mop. Immediately it flew out of the corner and twirled around the kitchen until the entire room was spotless.

Then she filled a giant clamshell with water, exactly the way she'd seen her parents do. She lifted the babies gently, took off their little outfits and fairy bells, and sat them in the bath. They splashed and kicked their legs, giggling at the waves they made.

"Okay," Olivia said, "let's get clean." She opened the baby soap.

Bubble after bubble rose into the air. The babies laughed harder, blowing the bubbles back and forth.

Olivia laughed too. *Pop, pop, pop.* The bubbles burst and cleaned the babies with a splash of soap.

"Are you ready to rinse?" she asked. "And

have some real fun?" The twins squealed with delight as Olivia reached through the knothole window and pulled a small cloud into the treehouse.

Olivia tapped the cloud with her wand and said, *"Drizzle, drizzle, soft and light, rinse the twins, and do it right."*

Gentle raindrops fell from the cloud and sprinkled the babies. They stuck out their tongues to catch the drops.

Finally, when the twins were squeaky clean, Olivia wrapped them in giant leaves and brought them to her parents' big bed to dress them.

"Now, let's see," she said, sifting through a pile of silky-soft outfits. "What should you wear?"

"Bye-bye, Wivvy," said Nicholas.

"What?" asked Olivia, turning around. "Oh, no!" The babies were flying out the window!

Chapter 7

Olivia raced after the fairies. She caught a glimpse of their chunky little wings disappearing around a corner, and then they were gone.

"They're not even wearing their fairy bells," she groaned. "I'll never find them." She flew frantically, asking everyone if they had seen two fairy babies.

"They z-z-z-zipped that way, toward Fairyland Meadow," a queen bee answered.

Fairyland Meadow? Maybe they were playing with Belinda, Dorrie, and Trina right now!

"Hey! What are you doing here?" Belinda asked when Olivia arrived at the weeping willow tree. "I thought you were working on your cloud."

"It's the twins!" Olivia choked out. "They flew away, and now I can't find them!"

A flood of tears rained down on the fairies. "Oh, no," sobbed the tree. "Those babies could be anywhere!"

"Don't worry, Mr. Willow." Dorrie patted the tree and nodded to Olivia. "We'll find those fairies."

"Okay." Trina rubbed her wings together, thinking. "We'll separate into two teams. Dorrie and I will look around the Magic Minimall and Pixie Skyway. Olivia, you and Belinda go to the Rainbow Bridge."

Olivia gasped. "The Rainbow Bridge? Do you think . . . could it be . . . that they slid down to Earth-Below?"

"Of course not," Belinda said soothingly. "But let's look just in case!"

The four friends took off. When Belinda and Olivia arrived at the Rainbow Bridge, silver-winged grown-up fairies were sliding down to work. A friendly-looking spider was directing traffic.

"Excuse me, Mr. Spider," Olivia said tearfully. "Have you seen two fairy babies?"

The spider held up six of his eight arms to stop traffic in all directions. "No, I haven't. Babies aren't allowed on the bridge."

Olivia sighed with relief. Thank goodness the babies hadn't floated to Earth-Below. She looked around and noticed the prettiest daffodil she had ever seen, beckoning with her leaves.

Olivia flew over. The flower opened her petals, and there were Nicholas and Natalia, curled up, fast asleep.

Olivia was overjoyed! She scooped up her baby brother and sister. "How can I ever thank you, Daffodil?"

The flower bowed gracefully. Her leaves swayed in the breeze.

"I know!" Olivia snapped her fingers. "I'll sculpt my cloud to look like you!"

Nicholas stirred in her arms. "We'd better get these fairies home, Belinda, and wait for my parents to come back," Olivia said. "I don't think they'll be very happy when they hear I lost the babies."

✳✳✳

All afternoon and evening, Olivia felt weepy. She had been so careless with Nicholas and Natalia! When her mother came to tuck her in that night, she was still in tears.

"How could I have lost the babies?" she sobbed. "I'm a bad fairy sister."

"Olivia, you are the best sister these twins could have. Sometimes fairy babies just fly away. Everybody in Fairyland knows that. And when someone finds a lost fairy baby, they hold the fairy and wait for its parents to fly by. Exactly the way the daffodil did."

"The daffodil was very nice," Olivia sniffled.

"I think three good things happened today."

"You do?"

"Yes. One, you learned never, ever to take off the fairy bells."

"I'll never take them off again," Olivia said solemnly.

"Two, you found an idea for your cloud shape—the daffodil. And three, you made the lovely sculpture of Nicholas and Natalia. I think we'll have to leave that in the living room for everyone to see."

"But, Mom, that's not good enough for people to see. It was just a way to keep the babies quiet."

"Well, I disagree. I think it's beautiful. Now go to sleep, sweet fairy. Tomorrow you must make your cloud."

Chapter 8

Olivia could hardly wait to go to her new art class. She wanted to work on her flower cloud. She spent most of the class shaping the first petal.

"Very nice detail!" Mr. Meadowleaf called.

Olivia grinned. Maybe she still had time to create a beautiful cloud. She wanted hers to really stand out from the others. She stepped back from her flower to take a good look.

"What a quaint cloud, Olivia. *I'm* doing a flower for *my* project too. Funny how you and I had the same idea," a familiar voice said. "Of course, I'm almost finished. I've been working on it all week."

Olivia whirled around. "Laurel! What are you doing in this class?"

"Aunt Magdalena asked me to say hello to Mr. Meadowleaf."

Mr. Meadowleaf looked a little confused. "I just talked to Magdalena this morning. Oh, well. Tell your aunt hi from me in return. And I'll talk to her soon."

Laurel turned to leave the art branch with a smug smile. "Actually, I came because I wanted to remind you," she whispered to Olivia, "that I'm going to win the contest, no matter what advanced art class you might take." She raised her voice and said sweetly, "Good-bye, Mr. Meadowleaf."

Olivia tried not to cry. She looked up at the

cuckoo clock. Class was almost over and she had shaped only one petal! She'd have to sit through the rest of her classes before she could go home and work on the cloud. Laurel would definitely beat her if she couldn't finish in time.

"Excuse me, sweet fairy."

"Mom!" Olivia lifted her head from her cloud as her mother floated into the art branch. "What are you doing here? Are the twins okay?"

"Everyone's fine," Mrs. Skye said quickly. "But your dad and I have a work emergency. A tropical rain forest has just been replanted, and we have to figure out dozens of tree heights. I have special permission to take you out of school. We need you to fairy-sit all day."

"Oh, Mom!" Olivia said, trying not to wail. "I have to finish my cloud today."

Mrs. Skye nodded. "I know. I hate to do this, but your father and I need your help.

We'll come back as quickly as we can. The twins are big enough to play by themselves, so you can work at home."

Olivia brightened. Maybe this would work after all. Excused from school, she could spend the rest of the afternoon and all evening on her cloud. "Let's go!"

***

At home, Nicholas and Natalia were busy playing tag with two ladybugs. So far, so good, Olivia thought, as she waved good-bye to her parents, then put her flower-cloud on the bedroom floor.

Bang! Crash! Olivia looked up and gasped. In the two seconds it had taken to put her cloud down, the twins had found her art supplies! Paint dripped everywhere—on the floor, on her walnut dresser, across her leaf-bed, and all over the twins. Nicholas was bright blue from head to toe. Natalia was red and yellow.

"Wook, Wivvy," said Nicholas. He flapped

one paint-coated wing. Blue paint sprayed Olivia's wall.

"Come here, you two!" Olivia reached for Natalia, but the little baby slipped out of her grasp. The twins fluttered to the ceiling, drizzling paint like rain.

Ding-dong. The door chime rang. "Oh!" Olivia cried. "What now?"

She raced through the house and flung open the door. "Hi, Olivia," said Dorrie. Trina and Belinda stood behind her. "We heard you had to leave school to fairy-sit."

"And we know you need time for the cloud contest," added Trina.

Belinda nodded. "We're here to help!"

Chapter 9

All afternoon Olivia's friends fairy-sat. First they helped the twins clean up the mess. Then Belinda took them on a super–speed flight to the meadow. Trina read them fairy tales. Dorrie made them laugh just by tripping over her own wings.

Meanwhile, Olivia shaped and pinched and pulled and twisted her cloud dough. Finally she sat back on her heels. There! She was done. Seconds later, the magic dough dried and hardened. The daffodil looked so real, so lifelike, Olivia almost expected it to talk.

I'm going to win, she thought. No matter who Laurel is related to.

"Hey, everybody!" she shouted. "Come in and look at my cloud!" She held it up, ready for her friends.

The twins scampered in first and raced right for her.

"Hugs?" said Natalia.

"Kisses?" said Nicholas.

"Wait," Olivia warned. "Let me put down the cloud. Or else—"

Crrrash! The twins flew straight into Olivia's arms—and knocked her cloud to the floor. Olivia gasped. Her model broke into a hundred pieces!

Chapter 10

Belinda, Trina, and Dorrie rushed over. The twins hovered by the ceiling, watching with worried expressions.

"Are you okay?" asked Dorrie.

"I'm fine." Olivia nodded glumly as she picked up the pieces. "But my cloud is ruined," she said in a trembling voice.

"Maybe we can tape it together," Trina offered.

"That won't work. There are too many

pieces." Olivia gulped, holding back the tears.

"We can just wave our wands and make it all better," Belinda said.

Olivia shook her head. "We can't. I had to use special dough. It's treated with fairy dust so no other magic can work on it." She showed them the contest rules. "This way nobody can cheat and just conjure up the best cloud. My cloud is ruined. Now Magdalena will never see my work."

Belinda sat next to her. "Just make another one!" she said.

"Good idea!" said Trina.

"Sure," said Dorrie, looking around. "Let's get more dough."

Olivia gazed at her friends. It seemed so simple to them. They didn't understand how long it had taken her to make her cloud come to life. A second daffodil cloud would never be as good as the first.

"I don't have enough time," she told them.

"The contest is tomorrow after school. Thanks for the help, but I'll be okay. I'll see you tomorrow."

"Hey!" said Belinda when she was almost out the door. "What is that?" She was pointing to the sculpture Olivia had made of the messy twins.

"That silly thing?" Olivia said. "I dashed it off to keep the twins out of trouble."

She hugged her friends good-bye one by one and waved as they flew away. Then she slumped on a kitchen chair and let the tears roll down her cheeks.

"Don't cwy, Wivvy," said Natalia. She wiped Olivia's tears with her grubby hands.

"We wuv you," Nicholas said, fluttering around and around his big sister.

Olivia gave a little laugh. They were being so sweet. How could she be mad at them?

✳✳✳

58

"We're so sorry about your contest project," Mrs. Skye told Olivia late that night as she tucked her into bed. "But we finished the rain forest. No more fairy-sitting for you!"

"That's right," Mr. Skye added, standing behind Mrs. Skye. "Now you can paint and draw and sculpt all you like."

Olivia knew her parents were trying to be nice. But it was too late for the contest . . . too late for everything.

Chapter 11

The next day in school, Olivia was quieter than usual.

"Where's your cloud, Olivia?" Laurel asked. "Did you decide not to enter the contest after all?" She laughed loudly. "Too afraid I'd win?"

"You hush up," Trina said. "It's none of your business."

"Of course it's my business," Laurel said. "I dare you to come to Fairy Hall and see me win first place."

Olivia pulled Trina away. She didn't want to get into any arguments. Especially now, when she felt so awful.

The day passed slowly. It seemed that nothing could make Olivia feel better—not star polishing, not rainbow painting, and definitely not her special art class, where everyone talked about the contest. Finally the last school bell chimed. Olivia's friends gathered around her.

"Come on," said Dorrie. "Let's go to Fairy Hall."

"I'm not going," Olivia said.

"Be a good sport and see who wins," Trina said. "Just because you didn't enter doesn't mean you shouldn't go. It'll be fun to see everyone else's clouds. And you can see what Magdalena chooses as the winner."

Olivia took a deep breath. Maybe her friends were right. Besides, she should go and congratulate the winner—even if it was Laurel. "All right."

When they arrived at Fairy Hall, Olivia gazed around in amazement.

The hall was lined with model clouds. Rows and rows of clouds—and almost every one was a flower. Olivia walked past pansies, roses, and tulips. One flower stood out because it was so . . . strange. Olivia stopped in front of it and stared for a few minutes. She was pretty sure it was a daisy. But the petals were all different sizes, and they stuck out in crazy directions.

"How do you like the winning cloud?" Laurel said, suddenly at their wings. "Aunt Magdalena always liked daisies."

This daisy is Laurel's winning cloud? My daffodil would have beat that even shattered in a hundred pieces, Olivia thought. But she didn't say anything. No need to argue. She kept walking . . . past more daisies and dandelions and lilacs. So many flowers, she thought. But then she stopped in front of one cloud that was totally different—her model of Nicholas and Natalia!

Chapter 12

"Wh-Wh-What's going on?" Olivia asked, confused.

Belinda grinned. "We entered your fairy twin cloud in the contest. After you were in bed last night, we flew over and talked to your parents. They thought it was a good idea, so we brought it to Fairy Hall this morning."

"I can't believe it!" Olivia exclaimed. She wasn't sure whether she'd win or not, but her cloud was fun, and full of love. She'd be proud to have Magdalena look at it.

"Wivvy! Wivvy!" Olivia wheeled around to see the twins, flying over for a hug.

"We're all here," said Mr. Skye, fluttering closer. "You've been so terrific about sharing the work at home. So we wanted to share something special with you."

Olivia hugged them tight. She felt lucky to have such a great family.

Then Olivia saw Mr. Meadowleaf flying down the hall, along with Ms. Periwinkle.

"Great work, Olivia," the art teacher said. "Your cloud is so original."

Ms. Periwinkle patted the twins' heads. "And you captured these babies exactly!"

Fairies kept passing by, oohing and aahing over Olivia's cloud. Then everyone stopped talking and stood back as Magdalena judged each entry. Olivia saw her stop by Laurel's cloud. Magdalena raised one eyebrow, then kept walking. Finally she came to Olivia's cloud. She squinted at it but didn't change expression.

Oh, well, Olivia thought. No matter who wins, I'm glad I'm here. I'm proud of my cloud. And my twins!

A few minutes later, Magdalena stepped up to a small stage at the end of the hall. "May I have your attention, please?" she said. "I'd like to announce the winner. The most original cloud, and most special piece of art here, which will become the biggest cloud in the Fairy Cloud Parade, is by . . ."

The hall fell silent as everyone gathered to hear. Laurel stepped forward, ready to accept the honor. Magdalena cleared her throat. "Olivia Skye!"

Laurel stepped back, her face flaming red.

First place! Olivia blinked, stunned by the announcement. She looked at her cloud, then at the twins, smiling in their parents' arms. And even more amazing, she thought, the twins are sitting still!

***

Over the next few days, Magdalena helped Olivia carve and mold her cloud for the Fairy Cloud Parade. The fairies fluttered above the puffy white cloud, pinching here, pulling there. It was so much fun to work with the famous artist.

When they finished, Magdalena stepped back to admire the cloud. A giant Nicholas and Natalia—with bowls on their heads and berries on their chins—seemed to giggle out loud.

"We're all done," Magdalena told Olivia. "This is a marvelous piece of art. Full of feeling. It's obvious that you love your brother and sister very much. Now all you have to do is lead the Fairy Cloud Parade."

Olivia drew in her breath. Lead the Fairy Cloud Parade! She pictured herself standing at the head of the procession . . . pulling her cloud string . . . and . . . and . . .

Something was missing. Something felt wrong. But what could it be?

***

The next day, Olivia hovered at the front of a long line of clouds. Cloud fairies bustled around, testing their cloud strings, getting into place. The giant Nicholas and Natalia cloud towered above the others.

The parade lined up on Pixie Skyway. Olivia turned to watch the other clouds. They bobbed grandly in the sky, sunbeams bouncing off their bright white puffs. Olivia sighed with happiness. She'd never seen such a beautiful sight.

"Whenever you're ready," Magdalena called to Olivia, "you can start the parade. Let's get these clouds to Earth-Below."

Olivia nodded to the band. Nightingales sang a march, a woodpecker banged a drum, and the crowd cheered loudly.

Olivia waved at all the fairies. She tried to smile, but something still wasn't right. Suddenly she snapped her wings. She didn't want to lead the parade alone. This was the most important thing that had ever happened to her, and she wanted to share it. She beckoned to Belinda, Trina, and Dorrie to join her.

"I couldn't have done this without my best friends!" she told them. "Or my baby brother and sister!" She flew to the sidelines, where Nicholas and Natalia sat in the baby flyer. She led them to the front of the parade. "Watch out, Earth-Below. Here comes my cloud." Smiling, she grabbed the cloud string in one hand and pushed the baby flyer with the other. "We're off!"

The Fairy School Pledge

(sung to the tune of "Twinkle, Twinkle, Little Star")

We are fairies
Brave and bright.
Shine by day,
Twinkle by night.

We're friends of birds
And kind to bees.
We love flowers
And the trees.

We are fairies
Brave and bright.
Shine by day,
Twinkle by night.

LOOK FOR MORE
FAiRY SCHooL
ADVENTURES
IN BOOKSTORES FALL 1999

The Best Book Ever!

Trina has read every book in the Fairy School library—twice! Why should she be stuck with the same old fairy tales when there are so many new, exciting books on Earth-Below? She's even heard that Big People's books are bigger than fairies. Imagine all those words!

Mixed-up Magic

Clumsy Dorrie's magic always backfires. Why is she the only fairy she knows who's not good at something? Maybe her fairy godmother can grant her a wish and make her special. But fairy fiddles! Dorrie's fairy godmother is even clumsier than Dorrie! How can a mixed-up grown-up help a little fairy figure things out?